I'd just like to welcome you to this book on behalf of cows everywhere...

First published in Great Britain in 1994
by Simon & Schuster Young Books
Campus 400
Maylands Avenue
Hemel Hempstead
Herts HP2 7EZ

Text and illustrations © 1994 Keith Brumpton

The right of Keith Brumpton to be identified as the author
and illustrator of this work has been asserted by him in
accordance with the Copyright, Designs and Patents Act 1988.

Typeset in 15/22 pt Palatino by Goodfellow & Egan Ltd, Cambridge
Printed and bound in Portgual by Ediçoes ASA

British Library Cataloguing in Publication Data available

ISBN 0 7500 1448 2
ISBN 0 7500 1449 0 (pb)

Keith Brumpton

TANYA,
Hoofed Crusader

Tanya in the rarely used
Cow·mobile.

SIMON & SCHUSTER
YOUNG BOOKS

1: How it all began

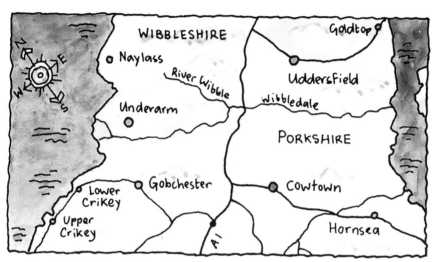

If you know Porkshire at all, then you might know the small town of Uddersfield, or maybe you can find it on a map. The story of the Hoofed Crusader begins there, one dark stormy night, on a farm high in the hills.

It was the sort of night when not even a rain-spotter would have set foot out of doors. The wind howled. It shook the trees. And there was a rumble of thunder overhead.

The cows at Owlhoot Farm had all gone into the barn to put their hooves up and have a bite of hay. All, that is, except for Tanya.

She'd found a particularly tasty patch of clover down by the stream and had decided to stay there for supper. The rain didn't really bother her. She swished her tail from side to side, as happy as a cow eating clover. (Which is not surprising considering that she *was* a cow eating clover!)

Back in the barn the other cows were
worried about Tanya.

"That Tanya had better watch herself."

"It's a nasty storm, she could get washed
away."

"Or just washed."

"Or struck by lightning."

None of which bothered Tanya in the
slightest. She liked storms. They were
exciting. More exciting than sitting in the
barn with Mavis and Beryl and the rest of the
cows.

Tanya noticed a delicious-looking shoot of clover over by the telephone kiosk. She stretched out her neck and was just about to get munching when the sky was lit by a blinding flash. Lightning! A loud clap of thunder followed, and then a crackle.

The other cows put their hooves over their eyes.

"Poor Tanya, she'll be fried alive."

"We told her not to stay out."

"This is very bad moos."

But, oddly enough, though she seemed to have been struck by the lightning, Tanya felt fine. Just a warm tingle all over her body. She noticed that her hooves were glowing with a strange light. And that the bell around her neck was still ringing gently:

"*Ting . . . Ting . . . Ting . . .*"

Most unusual of all, however, was the fact that she had begun to glow.

"Well, this is odd," she thought. "A Jersey Cow that's all-aglow." She looked around to see if anyone else had noticed.

Dr Rook hopped down from a nearby fence.

"Don't worry, Tanya," he croaked. "I saw everything and I think I can explain."

"You can?" asked the baffled bovine.*

"*Croak.* Yes. No problem. Basically you've been turned into a super-hero. The lightning struck your bell and now all that electric energy is yours. You'll be as strong as a hundred bulls. Perhaps even stronger."

* A confused cow.

Tanya wasn't sure she believed Dr Rook.

"*Croak*. OK, I can see you don't believe me. Why not try picking up that rock over there? *Croak*."

Tanya looked around but she couldn't see any rocks. Just one huge boulder.

"Yes, that. That's what I mean."

Tanya thought Dr Rook must be joking. Rooks were like that. Always joking. Joking and croaking.

"It's too big."

"Just try."

Tanya bent down and picked up the
boulder with her hoof. It felt like she was
picking a daisy. It felt as light as a bar of Aero.

"Dr Rook, you're right. I am a Super-Cow!
A veritable Hoofed Crusader! And I've got
special powers! Does this mean I'm going to
have a lot of adventures? Will anyone else
know about me? How long will I stay this
strong?"

But it was no use Tanya asking any more questions. Dr Rook had spotted a large worm on the other side of the field and was flapping off in pursuit.

"Give me a ring if you've got any problems! Can't stop. *Croak!*"

2: Friday night down the cow-shed

better weather

Tanya's unusual glow hadn't lasted long. And neither had her magic powers. No one but Dr Rook knew anything about the strange events of that stormy night in May. Now it was Friday evening and the cows of Owlhoot Farm were waiting to be milked by Terry the farm-hand.

← a recent photo of Terry

Although it was Terry's job to do all the odd tasks around the place, he actually wasn't much use. His mother had written a note telling him not to lift any heavy objects or to tire himself out. And since he was about as strong as a soggy biscuit he got tired pretty easily. This meant that milking the herd was about the only job he could do.

The cows all used to joke about Terry, but they liked him because he told funny stories and had warm hands.

That evening Terry arrived late, looking worried. He was carrying a copy of *The Daily Tail*.

OWNER OF OWLHOOT FARM KIDNAPPED!

■ Kidnappers demand large amount of cash

a report by our agricultural correspondant, Gloria Wheatsheaf.

"This is a terrible business," Terry sighed. "Mrs Hedgewort was the best boss in the world. She taught me everything I know . . ."

The cows looked curious.

" . . . How to lift a bucket. How to make a cup of tea. How to dip a biscuit . . ."

Tanya looked over Terry's shoulder to see if there were any more details in the paper. Apparently the police didn't have any leads. Just three sets of footprints and a ransom note.

"If the police don't find her the farm will have to close!"

Maybe this was a job for the Hoofed Crusader? If Tanya could regain her magic powers then there was a chance she could help free Mrs Hedgewort and save the farm.

But how could she get her powers back?

3: A call to Dr Rook

There was a long queue outside the telephone kiosk. Two squirrels were phoning their sister in Dorset.

At long last it was Tanya's turn. She dialled Dr Rook's number and waited. Sometimes it could be difficult to get a hold of Dr Rook because he was always flapping about somewhere or other, but luckily it wasn't too long before she could hear him on the other end of the line.

Tanya told him all about the kidnap and said she thought it might be a job for Super-Cow, if only she could find out how to regain her special powers.

"Dial 222 and start to moo," suggested Dr Rook. "Coming into contact with the telephone kiosk again might re-activate the flow of energy. *Croak.*"

Tanya began dialling as best she could. It wasn't easy with hooves. Whoever designed telephones, it certainly wasn't a cow!)

"Two . . . Two . . . Two . . ."

For a while nothing happened, but then, mysteriously, the bell around her neck began to ring:

Ting . . . Ting . . . Ting

And her hooves began to glow. She started
to feel her powers return ...

Super-Cow opened the door of the
telephone kiosk and flew straight up into the
sky. What a feeling! The air rushed past her
lug-holes and her udders wobbled. She
opened her eyes and saw Owlhoot Farm far
below.

Poem

A cow in flight

Is a very strange sight

You might think that you're seeing double

But flying at night

Without any lights

Is definitely asking for trouble.

Sure enough, the Hoofed Crusader only just managed to avoid a passing pigeon, and then almost crashed into an electricity pylon.

"Pylons and pigeons . . . I'm going to have to pass my flying test!" she thought to herself, whilst wondering whether to turn left or right.

The story on *The Daily Tail* had mentioned an old barn where Mrs Hedgewort was working before she vanished. If Super-Cow could find that she'd be right on the kidnappers' trail!

It looked more like a cow than a bird!

Experienced birdwatcher, Mr. Ken Eaglecliff.

Flask of hot tea.

4:   Ron works out

Bull-worker

Meanwhile, back at the farm, the rest of the
herd was in a state of excitement. They'd gone
to see Ron the Bull to tell him the latest news.
He was in the gym as usual.

"There's been a kidnapping," they mooed. "Our boss, Mrs Hedgewort. No one knows where she's being held. If they don't find her the farm will have to close!"

"And the police suspect a gang of wolves."

"And Tanya O'Dairy has gone missing," added Mavis – between mouthfuls of hay.

"No one has seen her since she was milked this morning."

"Allow me to finish training please, ladies," Ron yawned. "And then I'll see what I can do. Now, if you'll excuse me, I've three hundred press-ups to do before supper."

"Well, he wasn't much use," remarked Beryl, walking back to the shed. "It looks as if poor Tanya will have to look after herself."

5: Ground Control to Hoofed Crusader

The runway seemed to be clear. Tanya stuck out her hooves, lowered her head, and hoped for the best. When she opened her eyes she found that she'd just made a perfect landing.

She could see a series of footprints leading into the forest. Because she'd never been a Cow-Guide she couldn't tell exactly what tracks they were, but she felt certain that they belonged to the kidnappers.

The forest looked dark and dangerous, like one of Mrs Hedgewort's Porkshire Puddings. Super-Cow wasn't sure if she wanted to go any further with this adventure. Cows don't like forests. Not even Super-Cows.

But then she thought of Mrs Hedgewort being held captive, and decided that since she'd come this far there was no sense in turning back.

Thanks to her special powers the Hoofed Crusader found that she could see straight through solid objects. This was very useful. It only took about ten minutes for her X-Ray vision to locate a small hut in the darkest part of the forest.

Inside the hut she could see Mrs Hedgewort tied to an old sofa. She was being guarded by two foxes.

One was outside with a walkie-talkie, whilst the other one stood inside, next to the sofa. They both looked extremely fierce.

Though Super-Cow didn't know it, the two kidnappers were the villainous Fox Brothers, wanted on farms throughout Porkshire for a variety of crimes:

Taking chickens without consent.

Digging tunnels without a licence.

Eating eggs in a built-up area.

Not to mention kidnapping you-know-who . . .

ARTIST'S IMPRESSION

ARTIST'S IMPRESSION

The two foxes are dangerous and should NOT be approached.

6: "Foiled again!" (As the turkey said to the chef)

Super-Cow felt her hooves glow with
   strength.
She was as strong as Frank Bruno
And twice the length.

Though the Hoofed Crusader felt strong, she
wasn't exactly sure how strong she was. She
really needed a Users' Manual to explain all
her powers and how to activate them. Could
she do anything apart from flying and seeing
through solid objects?

She could hear the sound of leaves in the forest, rustling around her. Above, there was a spring moon. Below, some very scrunchy grass which made it difficult to move quietly.

In the distance she could now see the Fox Brothers' secret hideout (not that it was a secret any more). What if they were armed? What if they were dangerous? What if they were desperate? Worst of all, what if they were armed, dangerous *and* desperate?

Mrs Hedgewort was being treated very cruelly. She had been tied to a sofa with string and forced to watch daytime television.

"Turn if off? *Please!*" she pleaded, but the older of the Fox Brothers just laughed and turned the volume up a little higher. It was a cruel, toothy laugh.

Outside, Super-Cow was hiding behind a tree, ready to make her move. The only thing wrong with this plan was that cows are too big to hide behind trees.

The larger of the two Fox Brothers spotted her straightaway.

"Hey you! Caped Cow . . . come out here with your hooves up!"

Things looked black for Super-Cow. As black as a stick of liquorice on a dark night.

She came out from behind the tree. There was no room to take off. What else could she do?

Just then the Hoofed Crusader seemed to hear a voice from inside her cow bell.

"Point your tail and fire," it said.

The tail in question

Super-Cow felt this might be her last chance. She carefully pointed her tail in the direction of the fox, and squeezed hard.

A powerful ray of white light shot out from the tip of her tail. It surrounded the startled fox. He was frozen as if in a block of ice.

Even his brush was frozen.

"A deadly ice-ray," thought Super-Cow to herself. "That's useful!"

The second fox had heard the commotion outside, and crouched down behind the sofa, ready to make a fight of it.

"Don't come any closer, Hoofed Crusader! All cows are cowards, or haven't you heard?"

Super-Cow pushed open the door and strode into the no-longer-a-secret hideout.

"Super-Cow!" gasped Mrs Hedgewort. "Can I have your autograph?"

The remaining kidnapper was very
worried. He could see his brother outside,
looking like a Fox's Glacier Mint. And now
this huge caped cow had appeared out of
nowhere.

"Er . . . half-a-dozen eggs and I'll go
quietly," he spluttered.

"No deal!" snapped Super-Cow, and for the
second time she pointed her tail and fired.

"Nice work, Caped Cow!" cried Mrs Hedgewort, looking at the frozen fox imprisoned in a block of ice behind them.

"Would you mind untying me so I can switch off that awful TV show?"

She hadn't even recognized Tanya. Perhaps it was better that way.

7: Possibly the last chapter – I'm not sure yet

Super-Cow had swore Mrs Hedgewort to secrecy, and signed some autographs. Then she prepared to fly back to Uddersfield.

She'd stored the Fox Brothers in the kitchen, where they'd probably de-frost some time in early summer.

With a *Ting* of her bell and a glow of her hoof Super-Cow was airborne again, hovering over the roof.

It was almost eight o'clock in the evening and there weren't many cow-parking spaces available. The Hoofed Crusader had to land about half a mile away from her favourite telephone booth and walk the rest of the route.

Once inside the telephone kiosk she felt her magic powers slip away once more. Now she was plain Tanya O'Dairy again. Just one of the herd.

Everyone fell silent as she walked quietly back into the cow-shed and lay down on some straw.

What a day!

Mavis and Beryl couldn't believe their eyes.

"We thought you'd been kidnapped," they mooed.

"We thought Ron the Bull would have to rescue you as well as Mrs Hedgewort! *Moo*."

"Yes, have you heard?" added Eileen. "Mrs Hedgewort has been freed and everyone is saying that it was Ron who rescued her. He's so strong!"

Tanya felt too tired to listen to their stories. It had been a long and exciting day. Especially for a cow. Maybe tomorrow she would just have a quiet day in the fields, perhaps treat herself to a clump of buttercups.

Unless, that is, someone were to dial 222 and ask for The Hoofed Crusader . . .

Also by Keith Brumpton:

The Peeping Duck Gang series –
  The Case of the Phantom of the Opera
  The Case of the Missing Teeth
  The Case of the Dream Stealer
  The Case of the Killer Budgies
  The Case of the Yeti's Footprint

Look Out, Loch Ness Monster!

The Four-Legged Sheriff